Charlie the Champion Pony

"Darren, why don't you and Charlie go first this time?" Mrs Thomas said.

Darren couldn't wait. He liked jumping too. Before he'd got Charlie he had practised loads of times on one of the riding school's ponies. He urged Charlie forward and they broke into a canter.

Charlie felt like his heart was going to explode as they approached the first jump, and at the last moment he shied away . . .

Titles in Jenny Dale's PONY TALES™ series

All of Jenny Dale's PONY TALES™ books can be ordered at your local bookshop or are available by post from Bookpost (tel: 01624 836000)

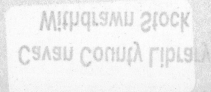

Jenny Dale's PONY TALES™

Charlie the Champion Pony

by Jenny Dale

Illustrated by Frank Rodgers

A Working Partners Book

MACMILLAN CHILDREN'S BOOKS

For all the children at 5 Collingham Gardens

Special thanks to Gwyneth Rees

First published 2000 by Macmillan Children's Books
a division of Macmillan Publishers Limited
20 New Wharf Road, London N1 9RR
Basingstoke and Oxford
www.panmacmillan.com

Associated companies throughout the world

Created by Working Partners Limited
London W6 0QT

ISBN 0 330 37469 9

A CIP catalogue record for this book is available from
the British Library.

Typeset by SX Composing DTP, Rayleigh, Essex
Printed by Mackays of Chatham plc, Kent

Chapter One

"It's Darren Drew!" a hushed whisper spread around the crowd. "It's Darren Drew riding Charlie!"

And they were off! Charlie was the best pony in the ring so far today and everyone cheered as he completed each perfect jump.

Darren sat back in the saddle as

Charlie cantered forward towards the last fence. The crowd held their breath. This was the triple bar that every other pony had failed to clear.

Charlie sped towards it and then they were up in the air and sailing over the fence as the whole crowd rose to their feet and stamped and clapped and shouted out Charlie's name.

"Charlie!" they yelled. "Charlie!"

Then Darren's name was being called out too – and he recognised the voice.

"Darren! Darren! Time to get up!" his dad was shouting up the stairs.

Suddenly Darren wasn't in the gymkhana ring any more – he was lying in bed. He remembered straight away that it was Saturday.

"Isn't it funny?" his dad said as Darren arrived in the kitchen a few minutes later, "how some people can be up and dressed and down for breakfast in about half the time when it's not a school day?"

Darren grinned at his father. "Today I'm taking Charlie for our first riding lesson."

"Really?" his dad teased. "I'd never have guessed."

"Dad," Darren began, reaching for the cereal, "I was thinking . . . if we had our own stable for Charlie, here beside the house, then he wouldn't have to stay at the Kings' stables and I could get to feed him myself every morning before school. That's what Tania King does. She goes out early every morning to feed Lady and sometimes she even takes her for an early morning ride."

"Well, Tania's parents have more space and the money to build stables," his dad said lightly. "Let's just see how you get on with Charlie first."

Darren knew how hard his

parents had saved up in order to buy him his very own pony. He didn't want to seem as if he was complaining. He tried to think of a way he could help. "You can cut down my pocket money if you like," he said. "And put it towards Charlie's feed."

"Oh, we've got enough to cover it. Don't you worry about that!" his dad reassured him. "How's Tania? I hear she's doing very well."

Darren pulled a face. "I don't know."

"You go to the same riding school, don't you? You may not be best friends but you go back a long way. You've known each other since you started school."

"Ye-es . . ." Darren was remembering that he and Tania hadn't exactly been best friends then either. Tania had pushed him off the rocking horse on their first day because she had wanted to ride it herself.

Tania was still just as competitive about riding now, Darren thought. Although at least she didn't go around pushing people off their ponies in order to get what she wanted. She didn't need to. Tania had won every junior showjumping event last year on her pony, Lady. None of the other local kids could ride as well. Except . . . just maybe . . . Darren. But Darren hadn't had his own pony then and Mrs Thomas's riding school ponies were usually too busy to be loaned to go to a show. And they weren't nearly as good as Lady!

Now Darren had his own pony he was sure Charlie would win lots of rosettes. Charlie was very special. Darren had thought so the moment he had spotted him at the pony sale. And it really was as if Charlie had picked out Darren too. Darren had been walking past Charlie's pen looking in the opposite direction when he felt a soft muzzle nuzzling his shoulder. He had looked up and there was Charlie.

"Dad, you couldn't have your toast when you get *back* from driving me to Tania's, could you?"

Darren pleaded as he watched his father reaching for the bread bin.

His father sighed. "You and that pony!" he said. "Never mind your poor dad's hunger pangs, so long as Charlie's getting fussed over!" But he was smiling too and already searching for his car keys. "Go and tell your mum we're off, then."

Darren went out into the hall and yelled upstairs. His mother appeared at the top of the stairs with a towel wrapped round her hair. "Wish Charlie luck from me!" she smiled. "It's a big day for him, you know – his first day at a new school!"

Charlie was stomping about impatiently in his stable, wishing Darren would hurry up. He remembered how happy he had been when he first spotted Darren at the sale. When Darren had stopped and patted him he had shaken his mane and nuzzled Darren's face, and then Darren had slipped him a piece of juicy apple. Charlie knew this was the owner for him. He was especially good when Darren tried him out and stood stock-still when they checked his legs and teeth and hooves. When Darren's father started to bid for him he'd hardly been able to stop snorting with excitement.

Going to his new home had been a bit scary but when he got to his stable he found that it was warm and comfortable. There was a deep bed of straw piled up at the sides, and fresh water, and Darren had given him a special feed.

In the next-door stable Lady pulled impatiently at her hay net.

Charlie had never met such a skittish pony before but he was getting used to her ways.

"Mmm . . . meadow hay, my favourite," whickered Lady, snatching another mouthful of hay.

Just then Charlie heard a car pull up and then a voice he recognised called out his name.

"Char-lie! I'm here!"

He snorted with pleasure as Darren ran up to his stable door and started stroking his nose and calling him a good boy.

Lady whinnied from her stable and Charlie heard the voice of Lady's owner, Tania. He didn't like Tania as much as he liked Darren. When Darren came to see him he always had a carrot for Lady too so that she wouldn't feel left out. But Charlie never got any attention at all from Tania. The

only time Tania had looked at him was when he had first arrived a week ago and she had come to inspect him with her father.

"That's a good little pony the Drews have found," Tania's father had said. "Better watch yourself, Tania. I should think you're in for some competition in the ring from now on!"

Tania had not looked pleased and she had ignored Charlie ever since.

"Hi, Tania," Darren was greeting her. "Are you and Lady going for a lesson this morning too?"

"Of course we are!" Tania replied. "Why? Are you scared we'll show you up on your new pony?"

"Show me up?" Darren grinned. "I reckon it's *us* who'll be showing *you* up, isn't it Charlie?"

Charlie neighed his agreement.

Darren went to get Charlie's saddle and bridle from the tack room. The saddle was rather worn – it had come with Charlie – but Darren didn't mind. He was just pleased to have his own tack.

"OK. Let's give you a brush then get you tacked up," Darren said.

Tania's father came out to see Darren off. Tania had already set off on Lady. "You'll be all right on your own?" he asked, glancing inside Lady's empty stable. "I told Tania to ride with you to Mrs Thomas's." He looked annoyed.

"It's all right. I know the way," Darren said. "Straight down the lane and first left."

"OK . . . Well, have a good time."

"We will," Darren grinned. "Come on, Charlie. Let's go and introduce you to everyone!"

Chapter Two

"Hey, Darren's got his new pony!" Sean Carter shouted, as Darren and Charlie turned into the gates of the riding school.

The others crowded round to look. "What's his name?" Sean asked, leaning forward to stroke Charlie.

"Come away now. We don't want to scare the new pony on his first day," Mrs Thomas said quickly, walking over from the stables.

Charlie snorted. He wasn't scared. He liked people and he especially liked people who made a fuss of him!

Darren patted Charlie's neck and told him how well he had managed on the lane when a noisy tractor had come up behind them. "You didn't get spooked at all!" Darren told him, proudly.

Charlie snorted again. "Of course not! When we're out riding it's my job to look after you, and I can't look after you if I'm nervous, can I?" Charlie had always tried to be careful – not that his last owner had ever seemed to notice. He had only ever spoken to Charlie when he got things wrong. So far Darren hadn't told him off once. Charlie hadn't done anything wrong yet, but somehow, now that he was with Darren, it seemed easy to get things right.

"Hello, Char—" Lady whinnied, behind him, but she didn't have time to finish because her reins were being tugged sharply by Tania.

"Come on," Tania called out. "Mrs Thomas has already set out the cones. I've got a gymkhana to practise for, even if some people haven't!"

All the ponies and riders

gathered in the paddock as Mrs Thomas gave them their instructions. "We'll start with practising bending and turning." As Mrs Thomas continued, Charlie watched very carefully.

Charlie couldn't help noticing that Lady was paying more attention to a tickly fly that had landed on her nose. She tossed her head about to try and get rid of it, then got distracted by a patch of long grass nearby. Charlie wished Lady wouldn't do that. When he hadn't paid attention his last owner used to get very cross indeed, and Charlie thought that Tania looked like she could get cross too. Charlie liked Lady and he didn't want her to get into trouble.

Tania and Lady went first. Charlie got the feeling that they always did by the way the others, including Darren, hung back to let them trot past. Charlie didn't mind. He wanted to watch someone else bend through the cones so he could spot any difficult bits and be ready for them. Darren seemed to be concentrating hard too as they watched Tania and Lady.

"Would you like to go next, Darren?" asked Mrs Thomas.

They both felt a bit nervous but they managed to clear the course too, and afterwards Darren was so pleased he gave Charlie a huge pat on the neck. "You did that really well," he whispered in Charlie's ear.

Charlie whinnied with pleasure.

"Well done!" Mrs Thomas called across to them.

Charlie was sure he had seen Mrs Thomas somewhere before, only he couldn't remember where. Still, it was bound to come back to him, he thought, as he turned to

watch the next pony and rider.

Over in the corner of the paddock Lady was getting more and more excited. Charlie could tell because she was flaring her nostrils and her eyes were especially bright.

"What is it?" Charlie neighed at her. Then he saw.

Mrs Thomas was now in the

process of setting up some jumps.

"Jumping is my favourite thing," Lady whickered.

"What's wrong, Charlie?" Darren asked, patting his pony gently. "You're all jittery."

Charlie *was* jittery. He could feel his heart going very fast, faster even than when he was galloping.

"Darren, why don't you and Charlie go first this time?" Mrs Thomas said.

Darren couldn't wait. He liked jumping too. Before he'd got Charlie he had practised loads of times on one of the riding school's ponies. He urged Charlie forward and they broke into a canter.

Charlie felt like his heart was going to explode as they

approached the first jump, and at the last moment he shied away.

"Never mind, Darren. Try the next one," Mrs Thomas called out to them.

By this time Charlie was giddy and the sound of his own hooves was deafening. Everything ahead was blurry.

"Come on, Charlie, you can do it!" Darren urged him.

But Charlie knew he couldn't make the jump. Not even for Darren. He veered away for a second time.

As Darren brought Charlie back to a walk, Charlie hung his head. He knew that he had let Darren down. Darren needed a pony who

could jump, and Charlie wasn't that pony.

Mrs Thomas came over to join them.

Darren listened very carefully to what Mrs Thomas said and when his name was mentioned Charlie pricked up his ears too.

"I think I know this pony," Darren's riding teacher was saying, frowning. "I was over at the Wilkinsons' stables, picking up some equipment I'd lent them when I spotted him with Colin Jenkins, his owner then. Young Colin was trying to force Charlie to jump when it was perfectly clear that poor Charlie was terrified. Apparently Colin had bullied Charlie into trying to jump far too soon, when he just wasn't ready." She paused.

Darren was looking very serious. "What happened?"

"Charlie rapped his front legs so badly that afterwards he was too scared to jump over anything."

"Where does this Colin Jenkins live?" Darren demanded, red-faced. "How could he be so horrible to Charlie?"

"Now, now," Mrs Thomas said gently. "There's no point in you getting all worked up about it, Darren. Mrs Wilkinson spoke to Colin's parents and Colin won't be allowed to have another pony until he learns how to look after it properly."

"That still doesn't help Charlie!"

Darren replied, angrily.

"No, it doesn't," Mrs Thomas agreed. "Charlie needs to get his confidence back. And I think you're the only person who can help him to do that now, Darren."

Chapter Three

Charlie was feeling terrible. What was Darren going to say to him? He could still remember his last owner's sharp words: "It's not fair! What use is a stupid pony that can't jump?"

And suddenly he was hearing those same words again.

"*What use is a pony that can't jump*?"

Charlie cringed. It was Tania.

"Charlie's a very brave pony!" Darren exploded. "He's brave even to try when he's been hurt jumping! *You'd* be frightened to jump again, if you'd been injured like Charlie!"

Charlie couldn't believe he'd heard right! Darren *wasn't* angry with him? Darren *didn't* think he was stupid and useless? Darren thought he was *brave*?

Lady stopped nibbling some grass and looked up thoughtfully.

Later, when they were back in their stables she neighed softly over the door to Charlie. "How

can a pony be hurt jumping?
Jumping is *easy*!"

Charlie quietly told her what
had happened. He was ready for
her to ignore him, but she didn't.
Instead she stood very still in her
stable and didn't fidget at all as
she listened to him carefully.

"Is *that* why your last owner

sold you?" she whinnied finally. "Because you were too scared to jump?"

Charlie neighed back that it was. "But Darren says he's never going to sell me. Ever!"

"When I was a foal I got left out in a field without my mother, in the middle of a thunderstorm," Lady whinnied. She shuddered. "I thought I was going to die. Thunder and lightning still terrify me. Tania's never ridden me in a storm so she doesn't know that yet. Not that she'd be interested."

"Why ever not?" Charlie was surprised to hear that.

"All Tania cares about is the next gymkhana," Lady yawned.

Charlie wished Lady hadn't

reminded him about the gymkhana. Mrs Thomas had given Tania an entry form but had said to Darren, "I think just the bending and flag races for you and Charlie this time."

Darren had tried not to look too disappointed, but Charlie could tell that he was. That had made Charlie feel bad all over again.

If *only* he could get over his fear of jumping!

There were only two weeks to go until the gymkhana and Darren and Charlie were out on the common next to the riding school. It was a hot day, so Darren was just giving Charlie some gentle exercise.

He hadn't tried to make Charlie jump again. Instead he had been teaching him how to bend and turn really fast. Charlie was getting very good at that. Mrs Thomas said he was the best pony at the riding school.

While the other ponies were practising over jumps, Darren had started setting out ground poles to mark out where the fences would be. He had already managed to get Charlie to trot over them.

Tania and Lady were out today too. Darren could see them practising jumping, over at the other side of the common where there were some logs. Gradually they got nearer and nearer until

Lady spotted Charlie and neighed a greeting.

"Hi, Tania," Darren called, but Tania only managed a smug smile.

"That Tania's such a show-off!" Darren muttered as Tania cantered Lady right past them and jumped over a low hedge at the edge of the common that led into Mrs Thomas's top field.

"Just ignore them, Charlie!" Darren said, protectively. "Jumping isn't the only thing that's important!"

But Charlie couldn't help wishing he could swap places with Lady, just for one jump, because the way she had soared over that hedge looked so exciting. Not that he would ever swap Darren for Tania under any circumstances.

"Come on, Charlie," said Darren, shortening the reins and giving a little squeeze with his legs. "Let's go for a canter!"

Just as Charlie moved off, a roll of thunder boomed out over the field. The sky had turned very black. Darren turned Charlie round to look behind them. The field where Tania and Lady were riding sloped upwards behind the common, and Darren had a clear view of the girl and pony as a second clap of thunder sounded.

"Oh, no!" Darren gasped, as he saw Lady rearing up in fright. He watched, horrified, as Tania was thrown to the ground.

"Tania!" he gasped, as Lady bolted down the hill. Tania's foot had to be caught in the stirrup, because the terrified pony was dragging Tania across the ground behind her!

Charlie neighed in alarm as Lady galloped towards them. Lady had to stop before Tania was seriously hurt! But Charlie knew that Lady was too frightened. With all this lightning and thunder, she wanted to get out of that field, fast.

"Come on, Charlie!" Darren shouted. "We've got to help them!" They had to reach Lady before she jumped the hedge!

But as Darren pressed Charlie forwards, he remembered that Charlie couldn't jump. Desperately he looked out for a gate but there wasn't one. He would have to dismount and try and climb the hedge himself!

A streak of lightning flashed across the sky and Lady neighed in terror.

Just then Charlie started to gallop! He wasn't scared any

more. All he could think about was his friend, Lady, and how frightened *she* must be and how he had to help, no matter what.

"Charlie! Stop!" Darren yelled, pulling on the reins.

But Charlie ignored him. The hedge was right in front of them now and there was no going back!

Chapter Four

Darren caught his breath as they landed on the other side of the hedge with a jolt. "Charlie, that was brilliant!" he cried.

But Charlie was too busy heading Lady off to hear Darren's praise. Neighing to Lady, he was trying to tell her what to do. Lady seemed to understand because she veered slightly to the right, which meant that Charlie could gallop alongside her.

"Tania!" Darren called out. "It's going to be all right."

But Tania didn't reply. Darren was frightened. What if she was badly hurt? What if—?

Charlie knew he couldn't stop Lady on his own. Darren would have to grab the reins. He galloped as close as possible to Lady. Now was their only chance!

Darren knew what to do. He reached forward and snatched at the flying leather straps. "Whoa!" he called out, pulling as hard as he could on the reins. "Whoa there, Lady!"

Just before they reached the
hedge, Lady stopped.

Darren jumped down
immediately and ran over to
release Tania from the stirrup.

Charlie nuzzled Lady and
whinnied soothingly to let her
know that she was safe now. Lady
was sweating and stomping her

feet. Charlie knew he had to get her to stay still while Darren helped Tania.

Tania cried out in pain as Darren gently released her foot. It was starting to rain heavily now and Darren knew he had to act quickly.

"Can you walk if I help you?" he asked Tania, knowing as he spoke that she couldn't. Darren knew that he had to call an ambulance so Tania could get some proper help. The nearest phone box was right across the other side of the common. It would take him ages to walk there.

Darren looked at Charlie. The quickest thing to do would be to ride there but that would mean

Charlie having to jump the hedge again. Clearing it the first time had seemed like a miracle. Could he do it again?

Charlie must have read Darren's mind because he started to trot towards the hedge.

"Hold on, Charlie!" Darren called out. He took off his coat and placed it over Tania. "I'm going to get help," he told her. "We'll be as quick as we can!"

He climbed up into the saddle and again he and Charlie flew over the hedge.

"You're the bravest pony in the world, Charlie!" Darren shouted as they galloped across the common.

Charlie didn't think he was the

bravest pony, but he reckoned he had to be the happiest. With Darren on his back he felt like he could jump over a double-decker bus!

Chapter Five

"OK, lad. We've got her now," one of the ambulance men said as they lifted a white-faced Tania onto the stretcher. "You and that pony have done a grand job!"

Darren and Charlie were both soaked through with rain. Darren had positioned Charlie to stand in front of Tania in order to protect her as best he could.

As soon as Tania was safely onto the stretcher, Charlie turned to look for Lady. He spotted her cowering against the hedge further along, too cold and miserable to try and gallop away.

The ambulance men had managed to contact Tania's parents and the riding school. Mr and Mrs King were on their way to the hospital, and Mrs Thomas had offered to come and fetch Lady.

"It wasn't your fault, Lady," Charlie nuzzled her, reassuringly.

Lady snorted, but it wasn't a very confident snort. She was still very shocked. Charlie hoped she hadn't heard the ambulance men making a big fuss of him and calling him a hero.

Lady blinked and tossed her sopping wet mane so that it splashed all over Charlie. "I thought you were too scared to jump," she snorted.

"I really *was* scared!" Charlie snorted back. "But you were in trouble and all I could think about was rescuing you!"

Lady gave another toss of her wet mane. "Really?"

"Well, you two have had quite a day," said Mrs Thomas when she arrived to collect Lady. She stroked Lady's nose. "Well, well . . . So you don't like thunder

. . . I wish we'd known about that."

"Will you be able to help her?" Darren asked.

"Well, we can try. With Tania's help, once she gets better." She took hold of Lady's reins. "Come on, girl. Let's get you home for a hot bran mash."

Darren gave Charlie a hug. "How about hot bran mash with extra molasses and carrots for you, too?"

Charlie whinnied his approval.

"That's Darren Drew!" Tania whispered to her best friend from school. Tania's ankle and right arm were in plaster and she wouldn't be riding for a while.

When Darren had come to see her in the hospital she had given him her entry form for the show-jumping ring as a thank you gift. Now she had brought all her friends to watch and cheer Charlie on. "Didn't I tell you Charlie was a wonderful pony? Today's his first gymkhana with Darren so he's probably a bit nervous."

But Charlie wasn't the only one who was nervous. Darren was, too.

"Just do your best," his mum had said, just before they'd left home. "And remember – the main thing is to *enjoy* it!"

That was all very well for his mum to say, Darren thought as he rode into the ring. Right now he was so scared that he felt like turning round and going home again.

But Charlie had other ideas. Now that he had got over his fear of jumping he couldn't wait to get out there!

By the end of his round he had knocked down one pole but Tania

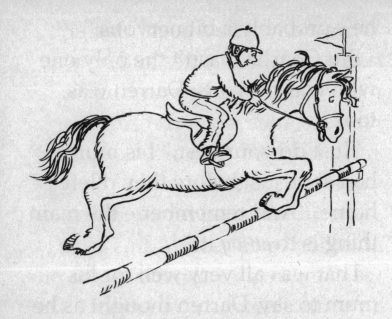

and her friends cheered just as loudly as if he'd completed a clear round.

When it came to the gymkhana races there was no one who could beat Charlie. He and Darren made a wonderful team, racing through the events with incredible speed and accuracy.

*

What a day it had been! Darren had won two rosettes and he was really happy. As he and Charlie received their second rosette, Tania hobbled forward to whisper something to the judge.

The judge asked for everyone's attention once more. "This year we want to give a special award to a remarkable pony and rider." The judge told the crowd how Darren and Charlie had rescued Tania and Lady.

Everyone applauded louder than ever as the judge asked the special pair to do a lap of honour round the main ring and presented them with a third rosette.

Darren was so happy. "*I* always

knew you were a champion
pony," he told Charlie, proudly.

"And I always knew you were a
champion rider," Charlie neighed
back.

PONY TALES™ No. 1
Sam the School Pony

Everyone loves him!

Becky loves Sam, the pony who lives in the field next to her school.
She's thrilled when her class are told they can look after him – and
ride him.

Everyone enjoys being with Sam, until something terrible happens.
Can Becky help her perfect pony when it really matters?

PONY TALES™ No. 3
Henry the Holiday Pony

Fun on the beach!

The best part of Andy's seaside holiday is riding Henry, the only pony among the donkeys on the beach.

But one day Andy gets a terrible shock – Henry and the donkeys have disappeared! Will Andy ever see his holiday pony again?

Collect all of JENNY DALE'S PONY TALES™!

The prices shown below are correct at the time of going to press.
However, Macmillan Publishers reserve the right to show new retail
prices on covers which may differ from those previously advertised.

JENNY DALE'S PONY TALES™

All Pan Macmillan titles can be ordered from our website,
www.panmacmillan.com, or your local bookshop
and are available by post from:

Bookpost
PO Box 29, Douglas, Isle of Man IM99 1BQ

Credit cards accepted. For details:
Telephone: 01624 836000
Fax: 01624 670923
E-mail: bookshop@enterprise.net
www.bookpost.co.uk

Free postage and packing in the UK.